PUFFIN BOOKS

Happy birthday, Puffin!

Did you know that in 1940 the very first Puffin story book (about a man with broomstick arms called Worzel Gummidge) was published? That's 70 years ago! Since then the little Puffin logo has become one of the most recognized book brands in the world and Puffin has established its place in the hearts of millions.

And in 2010 we are celebrating 70 spectacular years of Puffin and its books! Pocket Money Puffins is a brand-new collection from your favourite authors at a pocket-money price – in a perfect pocket size. We hope you enjoy these exciting stories and we hope you'll join us in celebrating the very best books for children. We may be 70 years old (sounds ancient, doesn't it?) but Puffin has never been so lively and fun.

There really IS a Puffin book for everyone
– discover yours tod

D0267439

Sue Bentley's books for children often include animals, fairies and wildlife. She lives in Northampton and enjoys reading, going to the cinema and watching the birds on the feeders outside her window. At school she was always getting told off for daydreaming, but she now knows that she was storing up ideas for when she became a writer. Sue has met and owned many animals, but the wild creatures in her life hold a special place in her heart.

Books by Sue Bentley

MAGIC KITTEN SERIES

MAGIC PUPPY SERIES

MAGIC PONIES SERIES

MAGIC REINDEER — A CHRISTMAS WISH

SUE BENTLEY

Magic Puffin

A Birthday Surprise

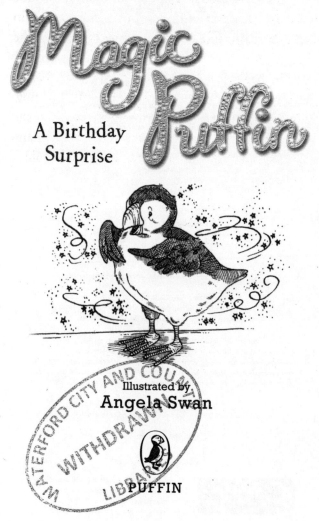

Illustrated by
Angela Swan

PUFFIN

PUFFIN BOOKS

Published by the Penguin Group

Penguin Books Ltd, 80 Strand, London WC2R ORL, England

Penguin Group (USA) Inc., 375 Hudson Street, New York, New York 10014, USA

Penguin Group (Canada), 90 Eglinton Avenue East, Suite 700, Toronto, Ontario, Canada M4P 2Y3
(a division of Pearson Penguin Canada Inc.)

Penguin Ireland, 25 St Stephen's Green, Dublin 2, Ireland (a division of Penguin Books Ltd)

Penguin Group (Australia), 250 Camberwell Road, Camberwell, Victoria 3124, Australia
(a division of Pearson Australia Group Pty Ltd)

Penguin Books India Pvt Ltd, 11 Community Centre, Panchsheel Park, New Delhi – 110 017, India

Penguin Group (NZ), 67 Apollo Drive, Rosedale, North Shore 0632, New Zealand
(a division of Pearson New Zealand Ltd)

Penguin Books (South Africa) (Pty) Ltd, 24 Sturdee Avenue, Rosebank,
Johannesburg 2196, South Africa

Penguin Books Ltd, Registered Offices: 80 Strand, London WC2R ORL, England

puffinbooks.com

First published 2010

1

Set in Adobe Caslon 14.75/28.5 pt
Typeset by Ellipsis Books Limited, Glasgow
Made and printed in England by Clays Ltd, St Ives plc

British Library Cataloguing in Publication Data
A CIP catalogue record for this book is available from the British Library

ISBN: 978-0-141-33039-6

www.greenpenguin.co.uk

To all Puffins, the feathered and the literary kind. You're Magic.

Prologue

'Yay! I did it! I delivered my first dream!'
Splash exclaimed happily. Flapping his
wings, the young magic puffin headed
home to Silver Dream Cliffs.

Ahead of him, dozens of his friends
flew in neat ranks as they also returned
from their special nightly task of
bringing good dreams to children

everywhere. Now Splash would be going with them every night too.

As the little puffin gave a joyful twitch of his stubby tail, a sprinkle of sea-blue glitter trailed out behind him. He was so busy thinking about telling his family the exciting news that he didn't realize he had fallen back from the others. With a flutter of his tiny wings, Splash flew harder to try to catch up.

Below him the sea was as clear as glass. Sand eels flashed enticingly among the waves. At the sight of them, Splash's small tummy rumbled and his mouth watered. He was very hungry after his busy night.

There was a strict rule that all magic puffins must return to Silver Dream Cliffs and report safely to the leader before they were allowed to go fishing. But those wriggly, delicious-looking sand eels were so tempting.

Surely it could do no harm if he dived into the sea and scooped up just one tiny beakful? *I could be back with the flock before anyone even notices*, Splash thought.

The temptation was too much. On impulse he dipped his wings and streaked downwards. The fresh smell of the sea surrounded Splash as he dived in. One, two, three delicious eels slipped down his throat before he quickly rose to the surface again.

But in that short time, the sky had grown much darker and the waves were being whipped into small peaks. There was a crash of thunder and lightning zigzagged across the sky.

A strong *whoosh* of cold air swept the little puffin up from the sea. Splash tried to fly up to join his friends, but he felt himself being pulled away off course. His heart beat fast as he flapped desperately against the furious wind.

'*Help! Help!*' he called to the magic puffins far above him.

But Splash's little voice was lost in the might of the sudden storm. It was all he could do to stay in the air and not pitch helplessly into the crashing waves.

Suddenly, there was a bright flash of sea-blue light and the little puffin felt himself drifting downwards on a gentle wave of sparkly magic.

Chapter One

'Bye! Have a great time on the island!' Martina Judd's mum and dad called, waving from the quayside.

Martina waved back. 'See you later! Good luck in the golf tournament.' Kids weren't allowed to take part in the competition, so Martina was going to spend the day visiting her uncle and

cousin on nearby Bird Island. She hung

on grimly to the wooden seat as her

uncle steered the small boat out to sea.

Martina could taste salty spray on

the breeze. She glanced nervously at the

choppy waves that slopped against the

side of the boat.

'I hope you've brought your sea

legs, love!' Uncle Andrew said good-naturedly, grinning.

'I think I must have left them at the hotel!' Martina replied with a wobbly smile. She was trying very hard not to think about how deep the sea must be now.

Her uncle turned back to the wheel and looked out of the cabin window. Suddenly, a *whoosh* of freezing water splashed into Martina's lap.

'Oh!' she gasped in shock.

From the other side of the boat

came peals of laughter. Martina glared at
her cousin who sat opposite.

'You idiot, Gary. That's not funny.
I'm soaked!'

'It's only a few drops! Don't be such
a wimp!' Gary crowed, wiping his hands
on his jeans. 'Your face looks green.
You'd better not be sick because *I'm* not
clearing it up!'

Martina swallowed hard, trying to
ignore the fluttery feeling in her tummy.
She wished she could think of a clever
answer. She'd forgotten what a total pain

Gary was. He seemed to think he could order her about just because he was nearly three years older than her. At least this was only a short trip. She wouldn't have to put up with him for long.

Martina thought longingly of the holiday hotel room, with its big squishy sofa and huge TV. She had planned to spend the afternoon playing on her new computer console. But that was before Uncle Andrew phoned and invited her to help him and Gary in their week-long survey of bird numbers.

Ahead of them, the island was getting closer. It was a dark looming rock, ringed with towering cliffs and topped by an old lighthouse. Martina couldn't imagine how Uncle Andrew and Gary could bear to stay there. What a total waste of the summer half-term.

Martina sighed, looking glumly towards the small open-sided cabin where her cousin had gone to stand with his dad.

'Why did *she* have to come?' Gary's moody voice complained. He obviously thought he was out of earshot, but the sea breeze carried his words clearly to Martina. 'She'll just be in the way. You know what girls are like about creepy-crawlies and stuff.'

'Now, Gary,' his dad replied calmly. 'I invited her, remember? It can't be much fun for Martina, having golf-mad parents and being dragged from hotel to hotel. I bet she has to spend lots of time by herself. I'm relying on you to make sure she has a good time with us. Right?'

'I s'pose,' Gary mumbled. He didn't sound convinced.

I don't mind being by myself. No one needs to feel sorry for me! Martina thought, a bit peeved. She liked being able to order stuff from room service and watch TV for hours on end.

And it wasn't as if she was a baby – in two days' time, she'd be nine years old.

The boat was passing a steep cliff face and big clouds of seabirds circled overhead. Others were swooping down on to narrow ledges. Their loud cries were deafening.

Martina wrinkled her nose. '*Phew!*
What's that terrible smell?'

'Seabird colonies all smell like that,'
Gary informed her over his shoulder.
'It's a mixture of fish, bird poo and
rotten eggs. Lovely!'

Uncle Andrew turned to grin at her.
'You'll get used to it. After a while you'll
hardly notice.'

'Oh great! Death by pong!' Martina
groaned.

Unexpectedly, Gary laughed.

Martina struggled to stop herself

smiling back. He looked much nicer when he was laughing, but she had to remember that he was still very annoying. She hoped that he might turn out to be friendlier once they were on the island.

Minutes later, they reached a small wooden landing stage. Uncle Andrew moored the boat and then Gary led the way up some stone steps.

Martina felt relieved as she reached firm ground at last. But as she looked round, her spirits sank into her trainers. The island was unbelievably bleak and wild-looking. Scrubby grass, low bushes and wild flowers stretched in all directions. Here and there, bare rocks poked through the thin soil.

As they all headed towards the old lighthouse, a cold breeze stirred Martina's short fair hair. She shivered, wishing she'd worn jeans instead of shorts and a T-shirt. But it had been a bright summer afternoon when they left.

'Hurry up and follow me,' Gary ordered. 'See those dark clouds? There's going to be a heck of a storm.'

'Yeah, right!' Martina muttered grumpily as he broke into a jog. He was obviously teasing her again.

Uncle Andrew took her arm. 'I'm afraid Gary's right. Summer storms blow up out of nowhere along this coast. Come on, love, we need to get inside!'

A fat raindrop *plopped* on to Martina's head, followed by two more. She didn't need telling twice. Hunching her shoulders, she dashed towards the lighthouse. They barely reached the shelter of the deep stone porch before a deafening crash of thunder rang out.

Martina hurried gratefully through the front door into a large bare room. There was a makeshift kitchen in one corner with a wooden table and chairs. Camp beds, a suitcase and a jumble of equipment were stacked against one wall.

Uncle Andrew produced towels from a backpack and then shrugged off his jacket before lighting a lamp and making them all hot chocolate. 'The storm will soon die down, but I reckon the sea channel will be closed for a couple of days. You'll be having a longer stay with us than we'd planned, Martina.'

'Oh no!' Martina stopped drying her damp hair and looked at him in horror. 'I can't stay here!'

'Sorry it's not posh enough for you, Your Highness,' Gary muttered.

'It's not that.' Martina bit her lip. 'I'm going to miss my birthday. And Mum's promised me a party and a big cake!'

'Oh dear. I'd forgotten that. You're

nine the day after tomorrow, aren't you?'
her uncle said sympathetically. 'I'm really
sorry, love, but it can't be helped. No
boats can travel to or from the island
until we get the all-clear from the
coastguard. I'll ring the coastguard, and
then phone your mum and dad to let
them know.'

Martina nodded silently as he went
to get his mobile phone. This was going
to be the worst birthday ever! To her
horror, she felt tears pricking her eyes.

'You're not the only one who's fed

up,' Gary said crossly. 'What about me? I'm stuck with you!'

Martina gave him a hard look and only just managed to stop herself saying something very rude indeed. She'd totally had enough of Gary and his mean comments. Whipping round, she opened the front door and stomped outside into the deep stone porch.

'Grrr! Gary is *so* annoying!' she fumed, slamming the door. 'I wish he wasn't my cousin!'

She stared out at the curtain of rain

that hid the island from view. Thunder rumbled in the distance.

Suddenly, there was a flash of bright sea-blue light and a twinkling mist filled the porch. Martina noticed glittery drops forming and gleaming on her skin – she could have sworn they were blue and green in colour.

'Oh!' she screwed up her eyes, trying to see through the shimmer, and wondered what could be happening. As the mist cleared, something whizzed towards her on

a big *whoosh* of sparkly air and *plopped*
at her feet.

Martina's eyes widened in surprise.
Looking up at her was a small
bedraggled puffin.

It gave a weak little gasp. 'Can you
help me, please?'

Chapter Two

Martina's jaw dropped as she looked at the exhausted little bird in total amazement. It had smart black-and-white feathers, a colourful triangular bill and little short orange legs. She'd only ever seen puffins in books, but she was pretty sure that real live ones couldn't speak.

She shook her head, trying to clear

away the confusion. All this sea air and upset was making her imagine things. This must be a baby puffin that had lost its way. How exciting to see one so close!

'Hello there,' she said softly, bending down. 'Did you get swept up in that awful storm?'

The little puffin blinked up at her

with bright intelligent eyes, which looked as if they were outlined with red-and-black make-up. 'Yes. I was returning from an important mission when I was blown off course.'

Martina jerked back in shock. She overbalanced and sat down on her behind on the cold stone floor. 'Oooof!' she gasped. 'You really *can* talk! How . . . how come?'

'All magic puffins can talk. I am Splash, the youngest of the Silver Dream colony,' the little bird with the

colourful striped bill told her proudly.
'What is your name?'

'I'm . . . um . . . Martina. Martina
Judd,' she stammered, still not quite
believing this was happening. It was like
some weird dream. 'I'm meant to be . . .
erm . . . visiting Bird Island with my
uncle and cousin. But I'm stuck here now
for a couple of days because of the storm.'

Splash dipped his head in a formal
bow. 'I am honoured to meet you,
Martina.'

'Um . . . likewise,' Martina said,

bowing her head in turn. She thought about standing up, but decided just to get to her knees, so that she wouldn't frighten this amazing little creature away. 'Did you say something about being on a mission?'

Splash shifted from one short orange leg to the other. The claws of his webbed feet made a scrabbling sound on the stone floor. 'Yes. Last night I delivered my very first dream to a human child. Now I am ready to do my duty and deliver good dreams every night. Magic puffins fly all over the world's seas to do this.'

'Wow! I never knew that dreams could be delivered or that there even *were* magic puffins. Where do you live?'

'Silver Dream Cliffs, on a beautiful secret island that is far out to sea,' Splash informed her. 'Human children sometimes visit our island in their dreams. But grown-ups can never find it.'

Martina listened, spellbound. The little puffin's world sounded so strange and magical. Her fascination was

starting to get the better of her shock.
'I can't imagine what a secret island
must look like,' she murmured, thinking
of how bleak Bird Island was.

'I will show you,' Splash said in his
gruff little sing-song voice.

He clicked his beak and Martina felt
a faint tingling in her fingertips as
Splash's feathers twinkled with sea-blue
sparkles and the porch filled with more
glittering swirls. Amid the mist, an
image formed and Martina saw a shining
island emerging from a crystal sea. It was

almost too bright to look at. Tall cliffs, topped with rainbow-coloured grass and jewel-like wild flowers, glinted in the sun. Thousands of magic puffins were waddling about on the cliffs or poking their heads out of burrows.

Everything seemed to zoom into fast-forward. Martina saw Splash gliding on the breeze above the cliffs. His feathers glowed a bright turquoise, and silvery-blue glitter streamed out behind him like a comet's tail.

As the mist faded, the magic puffin

colony disappeared. Splash stood there as a normal-coloured puffin.

'*Wow!* What an amazing place!' Martina exclaimed. 'I'm so sorry that you got lost in the storm.'

Splash looked at her with large sad eyes. 'I must get back. Will you help me?

Martina's heart went out to him. She knew exactly how it felt to be stranded somewhere you didn't want to be. 'Of course I'll help you. What do I have to do?'

Splash seemed to cheer up a bit. 'My

family will be looking for me and
sending magical silver fishing lines
through the sky. They are harmless and
invisible to most humans. But you will
be able to see them if you are close to
me. When I grab hold of a fishing line

with my beak, it will guide me home to Silver Dream Cliffs.'

'That's really clever. We'll keep a lookout for the fishing lines together,' Martina said, getting to her feet. 'Wait until I tell Uncle Andrew and Gary about all this! They're never going to believe it.'

'No, Martina! I am sorry, but you can tell no one about me or what I have told you,' Splash warned her seriously. 'Our important dreamwork must remain a secret from humans. You must promise me.'

Martina thought this over. She was disappointed that she couldn't tell Gary about Splash. Perhaps he'd think twice about saying mean things to her if he knew a magic puffin had chosen her to be his friend. But then she decided that if she *had* to be trapped on the island, it might be nice to have a special secret friend all of her own who needed her help.

'OK then. I promise. No one's going to hear about you from me.'

Splash clicked his beak gratefully.

'Thank you, Martina. Where can I stay that is safe?'

'You can stay with me,' Martina said at once. 'Oh . . . but I might have a problem hiding you. I think we'll be sleeping on camp beds in the same room as Ga–'

Suddenly, the porch door crashed open and Gary stepped outside. Martina's heart missed a beat. *Oh no!* He was going to see Splash at any moment!

Chapter Three

Gary scowled at Martina. 'Dad was worried that you'd run off, but I knew you wouldn't have gone far. Have you finished sulking yet?'

'I'm not sulking!' Martina said, nettled. 'I just wanted to . . . erm . . . be by myself for a few minutes.' She glanced at Splash's tiny figure in the corner of the porch. Luckily, Gary didn't seem to have noticed him.

'Whatever!' Gary rolled his eyes. 'Come on. Dad says you can sleep in the old lamp room by yourself. We'll be making do with the storeroom.'

Martina was surprised to learn that she wouldn't have to share after all. From the look on Gary's face, she guessed that he wasn't too pleased about it. Maybe he'd hoped to set himself up in the lamp room. She hesitated to follow him, not wanting to leave her secret new friend all by himself.

Splash seemed to know what she was thinking. 'Do not worry about me, Martina. I will come and find you later.'

Martina froze. What was going on? Splash had just given himself away in front of her cousin! How come Gary hadn't heard him?

Gary shuffled his feet impatiently. 'Come on then, you muppet, or Dad will think I've upset you or something. I don't want *another* earbashing about having to be nice to you because you're a soppy spoilt kid,' he drawled in a silly baby voice.

Martina could quite cheerfully have pushed him into the nearest muddy puddle. Instead, she gave Splash a tiny nod to show she'd heard him. Still feeling puzzled as to why Gary couldn't seem to see Splash, she followed her cousin back into the lighthouse.

Her uncle was busy with some equipment. He looked up as she passed him on her way to the staircase in the corner of the room. 'Feeling a bit better?' he asked kindly.

Martina shrugged. 'I suppose I'll just have to have my birthday a bit late. It's no big deal,' she said with a wry grin. She wondered what he'd have said if she told him about finding a magic puffin!

Uncle Andrew nodded. 'That's the spirit! Hope you like your room.'

Martina trudged up what felt like hundreds of winding stone steps. She expected to find a gloomy, dusty old room at the top. But the sight that met her eyes was a pleasant surprise.

The big circular room was built round the huge lamp that had once warned sailors about the treacherous rocks. But due to modern technology, it was no longer needed. The walls were lined with huge windows. Daylight flooded in, making everything bright and cheerful. There was an amazing view all over the island and the vast open sea. Overhead, the grey storm clouds seemed close enough to touch.

Despite herself, Martina felt cheered. It wasn't plush and comfy like her hotel room and there was no TV or en-suite bathroom. But there were sweet little window seats, a small table and chair and a cosy bunk, covered with lots of woolly blankets.

'This isn't too bad!' she said, bouncing up and down on the bunk.

A tapping noise behind her made her jump. She turned to see that Splash had flown up and landed on the wide sill. She opened the window so he could flutter inside.

'I like it here. It is a good place to stay!' he announced, after a quick exploration. Perching on one of the old lamp's huge ridged-glass lenses, he shook himself to dry his feathers.

Martina smiled. He looked so cute with his little domed head, bright eyes and friendly expression. 'Now you can stay with me without anyone knowing. Oh, and how come Gary couldn't see you in the porch?'

Splash clicked his beak mischievously. 'I used my magic so that only you can see and hear me.'

'You can make yourself invisible? I get it now. Cool! That's going to make things a lot easier,' Martina grinned delightedly. Being stuck here on the boring old island with her bossy cousin might not be quite so bad. Who could ever have dreamt that she'd have a magic puffin for company?

'Thanks, Uncle Andrew, that was delicious,' Martina said that evening, rinsing her plate in the sink. She'd just polished off sausages, beans and bread and butter.

Splash watched from where he was perched on the back of her chair. At first, Martina couldn't get used to the fact that only she knew he was there. But when her uncle and Gary paid

Splash no attention, she felt herself
starting to relax.

Once the plates were cleared away,
Uncle Andrew spread out a map of the
island. He pointed to the puffin colony,
which he'd ringed in red felt-tip.
'Tomorrow, we'll start counting occupied
burrows and plotting their positions.'

'Why do you have to do that?'
Martina asked, hoping that she wouldn't
have to help. Counting holes in the
ground sounded too dull for words.

'Well, there's been a gradual decline

in the numbers of puffins breeding on Bird Island,' he explained. 'My job is to check this year's burrows for eggs, so we get an idea of how many chicks we can expect. Each pair of puffins only rears one a year.'

'Only one chick?' Martina was surprised. She'd assumed they would have nests full of eggs, like the mallard ducks in the park that always had about ten cute fluffy ducklings swimming after them. 'So every single egg is really important?' she guessed.

'That's right,' her uncle agreed.

Splash cocked his head on one side, listening closely. 'Sometimes young wild puffins lose their way and visit Silver Dream Cliffs. We welcome them and share tales of our seaward wandering.'

Martina imagined the magic puffins and their wild cousins having a good chat. She grinned fondly at her little magical friend. 'I never realized that puffins were so interesting.'

Gary thought she was talking to him. He blinked at her in surprise.

'Well, I think they're amazing and so does Dad. But I would have thought frilly pink fairy dolls and stuff would be more your style,' he teased.

'That's all you know then, isn't it!' Martina said spiritedly. 'I hate pink!'

'OK, keep your wig on!' Gary joked, grinning. 'If you really want to know more, puffins are sometimes called sea parrots. They can live for as much as forty years. And once they choose a nesting site, they come back every year.'

Martina nodded slowly, deciding

that she wanted to find out all she could about Splash, his magical friends and their wild puffin cousins.

'Unfortunately, there's been trouble with illegal egg-collecting on some islands in the far north,' Uncle Andrew told her seriously. 'You can imagine the effect on a dwindling colony.'

Splash twitched his short tail angrily. 'That is dreadful news!'

'Why would anyone steal eggs?' Martina exclaimed.

'Beats me,' her uncle said. 'Some

people will collect anything. There are heavy penalties for stealing eggs. The police take swift action to arrest anyone caught doing it. Luckily, we haven't had that problem on Bird Island.'

Martina listened for a while, but as the conversation turned to lists of figures, she bit back a yawn. She stood up, ready to go upstairs.

Uncle Andrew handed her a torch. 'Are you sure you'll be OK in the lamp room, all by yourself?'

'Oh yes. I'll be fine now that I've

got –' She stopped suddenly, realizing that she'd been about to say that she had Splash as a friend. She would have to try a lot harder to keep his secret. 'Erm . . . now I've got used to staying here,' she corrected hastily. 'Goodnight!' Pointing the torch beam at the steps, she hurried up them with Splash flying ahead of her.

In the lamp room, Splash fluttered on to her shoulder. They stood looking out at the night sky, which was lit up by millions of stars. The young puffin's head moved from side to side as his keen eyes searched for glowing silver fishing lines. Martina searched too, but they had no luck.

'Perhaps I will never get home again,' Splash croaked sadly.

Martina reached up to stroke his smooth white chest. She felt a stir of affection for her little lost friend. 'Your family will keep looking until they find you. I know they will.'

Splash rubbed his soft head gently against her neck. 'Thank you, Martina.'

Suddenly, Martina spotted a plume

of smoke. It looked pale against the dark sky. 'Look! Is that a campfire? I didn't think people were supposed to come here without special permission like Uncle Andrew.'

'Perhaps they are egg collectors!' Splash squeaked, hopping up and down in alarm.

'Oh gosh! Do you think so?' Martina gasped. 'But I thought they didn't have any problem with them around here.'

Splash nodded, his eyes gleaming. 'We should go and make sure!'

'I agree. But we can't go tramping across the cliff tops in the dark. It's too dangerous,' Martina said worriedly. 'Why don't we wait until the morning? Uncle Andrew will know what to do.'

But Splash had other ideas. Martina felt a weird tingling sensation in her fingers as he fluttered down on to the window seat and his feathers ignited with glowing sea-blue sparkles.

Something very strange was about to happen!

Chapter Four

Martina gasped as a mini whirlwind of greeny-blue glitter spun around her. She felt tense with excitement. A warm tickly feeling ran up her arms and legs.

'Oh!' She felt an odd collapsing sensation. Her eyesight blurred for a second and then every detail of her surroundings became crystal clear. On the window seat, Splash seemed to grow in size.

Martina opened her mouth to ask what was happening, but all that came out was a startled little *squawk*. She looked down and went almost cross-eyed as she saw a bright orange beak.

She had become a puffin!

With a *whoosh*, Martina fluttered
across to land next to Splash. Her
webbed feet skidded on the cushion.

'This way! You'll be safe with me,'
Splash called, already streaking out of
the open window.

Martina zoomed after him. 'Oo-er!'
she yelled, flapping madly as she
exploded into the sky like a cork popping
out of a bottle. After a jerky start, she
soon got the hang of things and flew
alongside Splash. 'This is *so* cool!'

He glanced across at her with

approval. 'Follow me!' He swept downwards, trailing green-blue sparkles as together they skimmed across the waves.

Suddenly, Splash dived underwater. Martina paused for just a second before deciding to follow her friend. She whizzed along after his bubble trail, amazed to find that swimming was just like flying. The two of them burst out of the water together and headed for the cliff tops. Martina's tiny heart leapt in her white chest.

This was the best fun ever!

The cool night air rushed past them, ruffling their feathers. With her new keen bird senses, Martina could see every detail of the cliff tops. Clouds of insects were milling about. She'd usually be running for cover or grabbing the insect spray. But creepy-crawlies were no problem to her now that she was a puffin.

A number of wild puffins flew towards her and Splash.

'Greetings, friends,' Splash

chirruped. 'Have you seen any humans stealing eggs from your burrows?'

The puffins shook their heads, glancing at each other in alarm. They led Splash and Martina to the colony on the cliff top. She could hear the strange groaning bird calls coming from nesting puffins deep inside the many burrows. Martina wished she could tell what they were saying, but maybe she'd have to be a real puffin to do that. Others were flying in with beakfuls of sand eels.

Dozens of puffins waddled about:

some were rubbing beaks together and some sat with their heads poking out of burrow entrances. To Martina's delight, one breeding pair invited her and Splash to visit their burrow, proudly showing them a fat grey chick with a fuzzy head and big dark eyes.

'Oh,' she cooed in a birdie squeak. It was the sweetest thing she had ever seen. After admiring the chick, Splash thanked the puffins politely and the two of them left the burrow.

'We must look around for egg

stealers,' Splash told her, taking to the air again.

Spreading her tiny wings, Martina shot after him. She couldn't get over the wonderful experience of visiting the colony and the breeding puffins. If there *were* horrible criminals collecting eggs on the island, they had better watch out!

She and Splash flew back and forth, searching for signs of a campfire. But the thin thread of smoke had disappeared and after an hour or so, they still hadn't found anything.

Martina's wings had begun to droop with tiredness, when Splash gave a cry of triumph and landed beside a stamped-out fire.

Martina swooped down and landed next to him. 'Those ashes are still warm!' she exclaimed. And look at that.' She pointed to a few tiny fragments of eggshell. 'Oh, I suppose it doesn't prove anything. They could have cooked hens' eggs for their tea, couldn't they?'

Splash nudged at the piece of shell

with his beak. 'I am afraid not. See the small lilac-brown markings on this piece of white shell? This is a puffin's egg,' he said sadly.

Martina's chest tightened with fury. 'I knew it! Those mean people *are* stealing them! We have to find them before they escape!'

The magic puffin shook his head. 'No, Martina, we have done enough by finding this evidence. It could be dangerous to challenge the thieves and you are tired and need to sleep now.'

Martina opened her beak to protest that she was fine, but Splash was firm.

'Those bad humans are trapped on the island because of the storm. We can search again in the daylight.' Flying upwards, he led the way back.

In no time at all Martina was fluttering through the open lamp-room window. She crash-landed on her bed and warm tickly feelings ran up her arms and legs again as she felt herself expanding. The blankets were soft against her cheek as she lay on them.

'I'm a girl again!' Martina cried, pushing herself up on to her elbows. Her flying adventure had been amazing. She still felt all tingly and excited and was sure that she'd be wide awake for ages.

But when Splash snuggled up close against her neck and tucked his head under his wing, Martina had already fallen asleep.

She woke up with a start the following morning to find Splash sitting on her chest, nibbling her hair affectionately.

'*Phew!* Fish breath,' she giggled, fanning the air with one hand before gently stroking the top of his fuzzy little head. 'Sorry. Nothing personal.'

Martina gently moved Splash aside, leapt out of bed and threw her clothes on. 'Let's go and tell Uncle Andrew and Gary what we saw last night.'

The delicious smell of frying bacon met her as they came downstairs. Gary was sitting at the table eating toast.

Her uncle looked up, smiling. 'Did you sleep well? Sorry we couldn't provide you with a proper bed and a big soft duvet.'

'The bunk's great. I love it,' Martina said cheerfully, surprising herself. It was true. She'd barely given the posh hotel room a thought since Splash arrived. She adored her new friend. 'Listen, I've got something *really* important to tell you. There are egg collectors here. You have to report them . . .'

Uncle Andrew was all attention as she told him about the smoke they had seen from the lamp room, but she didn't mention Splash or their moonlight visit to the puffin colony. When she'd finished he stroked his chin thoughtfully. 'Hmm. Thanks for mentioning it, Martina. We'll check it out today, but my guess is that they're tourists with permits to look at the wild flowers and insect life. We get them here from time to time. Let's have breakfast, then we'll make a start. OK?'

'But they weren't just tourists. I saw their –' Martina broke off. She couldn't explain how she'd actually seen the campsite with her own eyes, after flying there as a puffin. He wouldn't have believed her anyway.

'I bet you were dreaming about that smoke,' Gary commented.

'I was not!' Martina bit her lip in exasperation. 'I'm right about those mean egg thieves. Just you wait and see.'

Gary rolled his eyes. 'You always have to be the centre of attention, don't you? What's it like, being a spoilt brat?'

'Gary!' Her uncle looked very stern. 'That's enough.'

Martina felt herself going red.

'Well, Gary, it's better than being a . . .

a . . . pompous know-it-all!' she fumed.

Gary looked surprised to see
Martina standing up for herself. Martina
even thought she caught a flicker of
respect on his face. But she was too
worried about the egg collectors to think
any more of it.

Tossing her head, she stormed
over to the kettle to make some hot
chocolate. An image of the cute fluffy
puffin chick came into her head. She

wasn't going to let those mean thieves
do this to Splash's wild cousins.

She had an idea. 'Do you think you
can find your way back to that
campsite?' she whispered to Splash, who
had fluttered up on to the draining-
board to perch next to her. 'If we show
Uncle Andrew those bits of eggshell,
he'll *have* to believe me!'

Chapter Five

'It's not much further!' Martina called.

'Are you sure this was where the smoke came from, Martina?' Uncle Andrew panted, as he clambered up a stony slope behind his niece and Gary. Splash hovered invisibly above them. 'I'm amazed that you could see this much detail from the lighthouse window, especially at night.'

'Oh, I have totally brilliant eyesight. I ... um ... take after my dad!' Martina blustered, playing for time.

Just then, Martina saw Splash dive towards the ground with an eager little cry. 'This is the place!'

Martina hurried forward and spotted some ashes and flattened grass. She felt a surge of relief. 'Look! Over here!'

Her uncle bent down for a closer look. 'You're right. Someone's made a campfire here recently. But there's no way of knowing if they were stealing eggs.'

'They were!' Martina insisted. 'And I can prove it!'

She began searching for the bits of puffin eggshell. Splash waddled about, helpfully poking under bits of dried grass and scratching at the soil. But there was no trace of any eggshell fragments. They must have blown away during the night.

Martina sighed heavily. 'OK, so maybe I *can't* prove it. But I just know that someone was stealing eggs. One thousand per cent! Please believe me, Uncle Andrew.'

'Honestly, you don't give up, do you?' Gary said. But for once, he didn't seem to be teasing her.

'No! Not when I know I'm right,' Martina said firmly.

'Well, I must say that you're one determined young lady,' her uncle said, shaking his head slowly. 'All right. I'll phone the mainland and tell them to send someone over to have a proper look around, just to be certain. But until then we won't know what the people who were here have really been doing. And it

won't be until tomorrow or later, when
the channel's safe for boats to cross.'

Martina was elated. She threw her
arms round him. 'Thanks, Uncle
Andrew. The puffins will be so pleased!'

Gary shook his head slowly. 'I don't
get you! One minute you can't stand
it here, the next you're like – top
puffin-protector!'

'So? Even spoilt brats can change!'
Martina sang out, grinning at Splash,
who was flapping his wings with
satisfaction and looking up at Martina

gratefully with his twinkly black
eyes.

She just hoped those campers,
whoever they were, would stay on the
other side of the island, far from the
puffin colony. With luck they had
already collected enough eggs and
wouldn't take any more.

As the morning drew on, the sun came
out. The cliffs were a patchwork of
bright green, dotted with yellow and
white flowers. Large numbers of gannets

and razorbills flew back and forth to
their nests on ledges on the cliff face.

Martina and Gary worked side by
side, helping to count and record the
number of puffin burrows. Uncle
Andrew carefully checked each nest for
eggs and chicks.

Splash perched on a nearby rock,

watching for a while. But then he told Martina he'd be gone for a short time and fluttered into the air. 'I will see you later!' he called.

Martina pretended to be shading her eyes from the sun as she waved to her magical friend. He was probably going fishing for sand eels and maybe looking for magical fishing lines. She felt a tiny pang of guilt because she couldn't help him this time, even though there was nothing she could do without her uncle or cousin noticing.

And what if Splash's family found him and he left without saying goodbye? Martina hated to even think about that possibility. She hoped like mad that Splash *would* return to her. Even though he'd only been her friend for a short time, she loved him to bits.

Swallowing a worried sigh, she went back to helping record burrow numbers.

To her delight, the wild puffins didn't seem to be at all nervous of her. They waddled around, making low friendly cries and didn't move away, even when she got right among them.

'It's very unusual for breeding pairs to allow you to get so close,' her uncle said. 'You seem to have a way with puffins.'

Martina hid a secret smile. Perhaps some of Splash's magic was still lingering around her and the puffins recognized her from yesterday's night-time visit.

To her surprise she was enjoying herself hugely. She didn't notice the smell any more and didn't even care that much when she stepped in something nasty. Martina's shorts were crumpled and had grass stains on them. There was mud on her knees too, but she wasn't bothered in the least.

Mum and Dad wouldn't recognize their favourite couch potato, she thought, smiling.

Later, as they were all returning to the lighthouse, Splash flew back with a whirr of wings.

'Hi!' Martina whispered delightedly, feeling a huge surge of relief as he landed lightly on her shoulder. So he couldn't have spotted any magical fishing lines. She longed to cuddle him, but her uncle and cousin were too close for her to risk stroking him, even though he was invisible. 'Had a good feed?'

He nodded, clicking his beak in satisfaction. 'I had a search round too. There are two humans hiding in some rocks on the beach on the other side of the island,' he told her. 'I swooped down and saw them putting eggs into boxes.'

'The thieves!' Martina guessed.

'I think so too,' Splash agreed. 'They had a boat, and it looks like they are planning to escape to the mainland.'

'Well, I hope the police get here quickly once the channel's safe and stop them!' Martina said with feeling. She wished she could tell her uncle about this new development, but there was no way to explain how she knew what was happening so far away. 'Anyway, those people are still stuck here for now. I guess there's nothing we can do.'

'That is true.' Splash settled down and fluffed out his wings.

'We were just going to make some sandwiches,' Martina told him. 'Uncle Andrew said he can manage by himself this afternoon. He told Gary he has to take me for a picnic – that's when you relax and share food in the open air,' she explained, as she didn't expect puffins – even magic ones – had picnics. 'You should have seen the look on his face!'

Gary was actually being a tiny bit friendlier. She decided to try to get on with him, as long as he didn't start teasing her again.

'That sounds like something nice to do. I would enjoy a picnic,' Splash cheeped, tickling her ear with one outstretched wing.

Once the food and drink were ready, she, Gary and Splash set out along the cliff path.

'Let's sit here,' Gary said, plonking himself down on a flattish stretch of ground with a stunning view of a rock face in the distance. He started to unwrap a sandwich and then changed his mind and jumped to his feet. 'I need some more exercise to work up an appetite!' he joked, starting to do a silly dance.

Martina was about to laugh, when she glanced at Splash, who had crouched down on the grass and spread out his wings. He had his eyes closed and seemed to have fallen asleep while sunbathing.

'Watch out,' she warned as Gary's capering brought him closer to the little puffin.

Her cousin laughed and pulled a face. '*Oops!*' He pretended to slip and staggered backwards with his arms spread wide.

Martina's heart missed a beat. Gary was about to flop down right on top of Splash!

Chapter Six

Pulling herself to her feet, Martina lunged forward. Grabbing Splash, she gently tossed him to one side and he fluttered to safety. She was still rolling sideways when Gary suddenly landed heavily on her leg.

'Oh!' Martina gasped as her knee twisted painfully beneath her.

Gary leapt to his feet. 'You idiot! Why did you get in my way?'

Martina thought quickly. 'I was just . . . erm . . . messing about. Sorry.'

'You're a strange one!' Gary gave her a funny look as he dusted grass off his shorts. 'Let's go up that hill. There's a better view of the gannet colony from there.'

Martina wasn't sure she could stand up without help. 'Um . . . I think I'll stay here, thanks.'

Gary shrugged as he walked away.

'Please yourself. I won't be long,' he called over his shoulder.

Splash shook himself and twitched his tail feathers into place before waddling over to her.

'Are you OK? Sorry I had to grab you like that,' Martina said. She bit back a wince. Her sore knee was throbbing horribly and making her feel quite sick.

'I am fine. Thank you for saving me from being squashed. But you are hurt,' he worriedly chirped. 'I will make you better.'

Martina felt a tingling sensation in her fingers as Splash leant forward, opened his beak and breathed out a sparkling pale-green mist that shimmered with what looked like thousands of tiny rainbow feathers. The mist swirled around her knee for a few seconds before seeming to sink into her skin and disappear. The pain grew hot for a moment and then drained away, just as if she had poured it out on to the grass.

'Oh, wow! It feels much better now. Thanks, Splash!' Martina reached out her cupped hands and the little puffin hopped into them. She drew him close, stroking his soft feathers and breathing in their clean smell of fresh air and salt. 'I love having you for my friend. I wish you could stay with me forever.'

She couldn't imagine life without Splash now. For the first time, she realized that maybe she wasn't that happy being by herself so much in hotel rooms. It might be nice to have a friend to do things with while her parents played golf.

Splash was nibbling a fold of her T-shirt affectionately. Suddenly, a shining silver thread appeared briefly in mid-air.

He stiffened. 'A magical fishing line!' The thread glistened and hung there briefly, but disappeared before Splash could fly up and reach for it. 'Oh! I missed it,' he cried in disappointment.

'Maybe that's not so bad,' Martina said gently. 'You could always stay with me. I'll be going home with Mum and Dad soon. Our house has got a big pond and everything.'

Splash shook his head. 'I am sorry, Martina, but that is not possible. I must continue my task of bringing good dreams to children with the other magic puffins. I hope you understand.'

'I do.' Martina swallowed the lump in her throat. 'I suppose I knew that really.'

'If my family send another closer fishing line, I may have to leave quickly without saying goodbye,' he chirruped seriously.

Martina nodded, fighting back her sadness – she had tried so hard to push the horrible thought that Splash wouldn't be staying, out of her head. She decided to try even harder to enjoy every moment of the time they had left together. 'Here's Gary now.' Martina said, smiling bravely. 'Let's finish our picnic. Do you fancy a bit of tuna sandwich?'

'It's my birthday tomorrow and I'll be going back to the hotel in time for my party, after all,' Martina told Splash as she got ready for bed that night. Her uncle had just checked with the coastguard and had been told that boats could use the channel in the morning.

'That is good news.' Splash sounded happy on her behalf.

But Martina was surprised to find she wasn't that keen to be leaving now. Splash still needed her to help him find his way home to his family. What would happen to her friend if he never managed to grab one of the fishing lines and find his way back to Silver Dream Cliffs? He could be stranded on Bird Island forever.

She still felt troubled as she got into her bunk and snuggled under a blanket, but she was too tired to think about it any more right now. Her eyes drooped as Splash flew over to roost on her pillow.

'Goodnight,' she said sleepily, kissing Splash on top of his velvety head.

'Sweet dreams, Martina.'

The next morning, it was just starting to get light when she woke with a start to find Splash hopping up and down on her excitedly.

'Martina! The puffin colony is in danger. I had a bad feeling, so I went to check on them. The egg thieves are there now!'

Martina sat bolt upright. 'Oh no! We have to stop them! What can we do?'

'I have an idea. I will be back soon,' Splash declared, fluttering over to the window.

'Be careful!' Martina cried worriedly as he opened it and then zoomed into the sky in a trail of greeny-blue sparks. She felt a bit disappointed that he hadn't made her into a puffin again, but she knew he must have a different plan in mind. 'I'll meet you at the colony!' she called after him.

She dressed at the speed of light and then hurried downstairs on tiptoe. Anger churned inside her as she thought of how many more breeding puffins would be robbed of chicks because of the mean thieves!

Just as she reached the outside door, she felt a hand on her arm.

'Oh!' Martina gasped, cold with shock.

It was Gary and he was already dressed. 'Where are you going?' he challenged in a whisper.

'To the puffin colony. The egg collectors are back.'

'What? How can you possibly know tha–'

'There's no time to explain,' Martina interrupted. 'I promise that I'm not making this up. I have to try to stop them.'

Gary took one look at her tense face. 'OK. I'm coming too.'

Martina didn't waste time arguing. Together, she and Gary raced along the cliff tops.

As they drew close to the colony, they glimpsed two shadowy male figures. One of them was kneeling near a burrow. A second man was carefully putting something into a wooden box.

'Hey! Stop that!' Martina yelled, too angry to think straight. 'Don't you know it's against the law to steal eggs?'

The man near the box straightened. Martina saw he was tall and burly-looking. He gave them a hard look. 'It's just a couple of kids,' he called to his friend.

'They must be with someone. Get them!' ordered the other man.

Martina swallowed nervously as the big man took a few steps towards them. Her heart was thumping hard. She could see that Gary was scared too. But both of them held their ground.

The egg thieves came closer.

Suddenly, there was a terrific squawking and loud flapping of wings. The dawn sky darkened as thousands of puffins, gannets and razorbills flocked towards the colony. Leading them was a tiny figure. It glowed like a green-blue comet and a long trail of brilliant shining sparks streamed out behind it.

'Splash!' Martina cried.

All at once a deluge of smelly sand eels, rotten eggs and other nastier smelly stuff rained down on to the egg thieves as the seabirds dropped them.

'What's happening?' Gary's mouth dropped open in puzzlement.

'It's payback time!' Martina said triumphantly. 'Yay! Go, Splash!' she said quietly to herself.

'Urgh! Yuck! Arrgh!' the men spluttered, holding their arms over their heads. They left the box of eggs and staggered away as fast as they could across the cliffs. The huge flock of birds followed, still pelting them with pongy stuff and diving down to drive them away with jabs from their sharp beaks.

'Amazing! I've never seen different birds flocking together to act like this before!' Gary was still staring, wide-eyed, at the spectacle.

He and Martina ran towards the sloping path the men had disappeared down. It led to a cove below. There was a small boat moored there, with another box between the seats. The two men, still pursued by angry birds, threw themselves into the boat and began rowing like mad.

'They're getting away!' Martina cried.

'No, they're not – look!' Gary

pointed at a police launch that was just rounding the cliffs. They must have arrived to check out the island after Uncle Andrew's enquiry. As Martina and Gary shouted and pointed towards the thieves, the launch veered sideways to intercept the rowing boat.

'Yay, just in time! Those men are toast!' Gary yelled triumphantly. 'I'm going to fetch Dad – he *has* to see this!'

As Gary ran back towards the lighthouse, Splash appeared in his normal colours and landed on Martina's shoulder in a shower of invisible sparks.

'That was fantastic. Well done, Splash!
You and your friends really showed
those mean thieves.'

'I am glad that the colony is safe
now.' Splash nuzzled into her neck.

Martina smiled as she felt him gently
nibbling a lock of her hair. She was just
reaching up to stroke him when a shining
silver line came looping towards them
from the sky. The moment she had been
both hoping for and dreading was here.

'My family have found me!'

There was a bright flash and, for the last time, Splash's feathers turned a bright glittering turquoise and a long trail of silvery-blue sparkles flowed out behind him. Seen so close up, he looked magnificent and regal.

Flapping strongly he whooshed out of Martina's arms and flew towards the fishing line.

'Goodbye, Splash. I'll never forget you!' Martina called, her voice breaking.

'I will not forget you, either. You are a very special friend. Farewell!' Splash called. He grasped the magical fishing line in his beak and was instantly whisked out of sight.

A single turquoise sparkle floated down towards Martina. She put out her hand and it landed gently on her palm. As she watched, it turned into a tiny bright blue seashell. She slipped it into her pocket, knowing she would keep it always to remind her of the wonderful adventure she and her magic puffin, Splash, had shared.

Martina stood there for a while,

unable to believe that all of this had happened so fast. Her heart ached, but she was glad Splash would be reunited with his family and able to continue his magical task of bringing good dreams to children everywhere.

She brushed away a tear. At least she'd had a chance to say goodbye. 'Take care, Splash. And give my love to the other magic puffins!'

Uncle Andrew and Gary ran up to her as they all watched the police team arrest the egg collectors.

'I hope they're put in prison for a
hundred years!' Gary said.

'Me too!' Martina agreed.

Uncle Andrew smiled at them. 'You
two have a lot in common, you know.

You've been a great team over the last few days.'

Gary gave Martina a playful nudge. 'Yeah, I reckon we have.' He took a crumpled hand-made card out of his pocket. 'Happy birthday!'

'Aw, thanks,' Martina said, touched. This had to be the strangest birthday ever. She was actually sorry to be leaving the island – after all the excitement it suddenly didn't seem like much fun to spend a quiet birthday at the hotel with her parents.

'Mum's promised me a hu-uge birthday cake,' she said with a smile. 'Do you and Uncle Andrew fancy helping me eat it?' Wherever Splash was, she knew he'd be clicking his little beak with approval.

Bright and shiny and sizzling with fun stuff . . .

puffin.co.uk

WEB FUN

UNIQUE and exclusive digital content!
Podcasts, photos, Q&A, Day in the Life of, interviews
and much more, from Eoin Colfer, Cathy Cassidy,
Allan Ahlberg and Meg Rosoff to Lynley Dodd!

WEB NEWS

The **Puffin Blog** is packed with posts and photos from
Puffin HQ and special guest bloggers. You can also sign up
to our monthly newsletter **Puffin Beak Speak**

WEB CHAT

Discover something new EVERY month –
books, competitions and treats galore

WEBBED FEET

(Puffins have funny little feet and
brightly coloured beaks)

Point your mouse our way today!

It all started with a Scarecrow.

Puffin is seventy years old.
Sounds ancient, doesn't it? But Puffin has never been
so lively. We're always on the lookout for the next big
idea, which is how it began all those years ago.

Penguin Books was a big idea from the mind of
a man called Allen Lane, who in 1935 invented
the quality paperback and changed the world.
And from great Penguins, great Puffins grew,
changing the face of children's books forever.

The first four Puffin Picture Books were hatched in 1940 and the
first Puffin story book featured a man with broomstick arms called
Worzel Gummidge. In 1967 Kaye Webb, Puffin Editor, started the
Puffin Club, promising to 'make children into readers'.
She kept that promise and over 200,000 children became
devoted Puffineers through their quarterly instalments of
Puffin Post, which is now back for a new generation.

Many years from now, we hope you'll look back and
remember Puffin with a smile. **No matter what your age**
or what you're into, there's a Puffin for everyone.
The possibilities are endless, but one thing is for sure:
whether it's a picture book or a paperback, a sticker book
or a hardback, **if it's got that little Puffin**
on it – it's bound to be good.